PETERRIFIC

WRITTEN AND ILLUSTRATED BY

Victoria Kann

HARPER

An Imprint of HarperCollinsPublishers

Peterrific
Copyright © 2017 by Victoria Kann

Based on the HarperCollins book *Pinkalicious* written by
Victoria Kann and Elizabeth Kann, illustrated by Victoria Kann.

Library of Congress Control Number: 2016936035
ISBN 978-0-06-256356-9 (trade bdg.) — ISBN 978-0-06-256357-6 (lib. bdg.)

The artist used mixed media to create the digital illustrations for this book.
Typography by Rachel Zegar
17 18 19 20 21 SCP 10 9 8 7 6 5 4 3 2 1
❖
First Edition

I put a block on the top of my tower.

"Pinkalicious, do you have any blocks?" I asked my sister.
"I am about to run out."

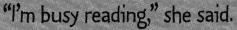

"I'm busy reading," she said.

"I want to build a GIANT tower all by myself! I never get to do anything by myself. It will be so tall that I will be able to get a star from the sky and give it to Mommy," I said.

"Wow, I want a star too! Can you get one for me?" asked Pinkalicious. "We can borrow some blocks from next door. I'll go get them."

While she was gone, I made drawings of the tower that I was going to build. If it was tall enough, it could go out the window and right up through the clouds. Then I could stand on a cloud and look below.

"Here are some more blocks! Are you really going to make it all by yourself?" asked Pinkalicious.

"Yes," I said. I got to work.

The tower got taller. I used tape, rope, and glue to hold it together.

"I need more blocks!" I said.

"Okay, I will ask the other neighbors if they have any," said Pinkalicious.

I used whatever I could find, including furniture. My tower got bigger and bigger.

"Look at all the blocks that I was able to find! But how will I get them up to you now?" asked Pinkalicious.

I knotted blankets together. I tied a basket to the blankets and lowered it down to Pinkalicious.

"Put the blocks in the basket, please. Can you get my telescope? I'll need it if I make it all the way to the moon. I want to see if it is actually made of cheese," I said.

"What kind of cheese . . . Swiss cheese? Cheddar? Parmesan? Here are some crackers just in case!" said Pinkalicious.

"PETER! What are you doing? That doesn't look safe!" said Mommy.

"PETER, come down right NOW!" Daddy shouted, grabbing a ladder, but it was too short to reach me.

Mommy and Daddy did not look happy.

"Don't worry," I said. "I'll be back soon. I just need to finish my tower."

When I finished my tower I looked down. Everything looked small, but the sky looked big and bright. I felt like I could see the whole universe!

I liked it here. I was way up high. I couldn't hear Mommy and Daddy anymore.

I didn't have any chores in my tower. No one could tell me what to do. It was nice not having to share my toys. And I had built the tower all by myself! I knew I could do it! My tower was PERFECT!

I tried to reach for a shooting star, but it was too far away.
I had forgotten to bring my net to catch it. I looked through my
telescope.

"Pinkalicious, the moon is NOT made out of cheese!" I yelled
with excitement.

Then I remembered that I was all alone.

It was dark. I was cold. I ate the crackers that Pinkalicious had given me. I realized my perfect tower had a problem. There was no way for me to get down.

Suddenly, I heard a loud creak.

Then a crack.

What if the tower fell down? I was getting sleepy. I will figure it out tomorrow. I wrapped a blanket around me.

"I am NOT going to cry," I said to myself, wiping away a little drop of liquid from the corner of my eye.

In the morning I could feel the tower
swaying back and forth. Uh-oh, it was going
to fall down.

"Won't you give me a ride, Mr. Bird?" I asked
a bird flying by. The bird kept flying. I needed
an idea.

"I know!" I said to myself. "I can tie
the blankets together and make a great
big parachute!"

Luckily I was an expert knot tier.
After I tied the blankets together, I
took some rope off the tower and
tied it to the blankets and then to
me. I used the basket as my helmet.

I needed to be very brave. "What would
Pinkalicious do if she were here?" I wondered.
I took a big breath and closed my eyes.
"Think Pink!" I said, and jumped!

I floated down through the sky, somersaulting through the clouds.

I landed right onto
our trampoline.

I bounced up,
then I bounced down,
then up again and
then down.

"Wheeeeeee!" I yelled with glee.
I was home again.

CRASH! The tower fell to the ground.

Luckily no one was hurt.

"Mommy and Daddy," I said, "I am sorry. I promise not to build anything ever again."

"What?! You are a good builder. In fact, you *should* build it again!" said Daddy.

"Really?!" I said happily.

"Your next tower should be a little smaller and safer, and you will definitely need a proper way to get down," said Mommy.

"I'll build a new tower, and it will have an elevator powered by the wind as the way to get up to the top and a slide as the way to get down!" I said. "And this time Pinkalicious is coming with me, and together we are going to catch a shooting star!"

"I can't wait, Peter. You are the best brother in the world. In fact, you are Peterrific!" said Pinkalicious.